# TOM PERCIVAL
# BILLY'S BRAVERY

D1151331

This book belongs to:

------------------------------------------------

I am a reader and I celebrated World Book Day
2023 with this gift from my local bookseller
and Bloomsbury Children's Books

## WORLD BOOK DAY®

**World Book Day's** mission is to offer every child and young person the opportunity
to read and love books by giving you the chance to have a book of your own.

To find out more, and for fun activities including the monthly World Book Day Book Club,
video stories and book recommendations, visit **worldbookday.com**

**World Book Day** is a charity sponsored by National Book Tokens.

BLOOMSBURY
CHILDREN'S BOOKS
LONDON  OXFORD  NEW YORK  NEW DELHI  SYDNEY

# Billy absolutely LOVED Nature Girl!
## She was the BRAVEST
## superhero of all.

He had read the books, watched
the cartoons . . .

And he'd even made a Nature Girl costume!
So on World Book Day . . .

Billy knew exactly who he
wanted to dress up as.

But then a voice inside Billy's head whispered,
"You can't dress as *Nature Girl* – you'll look silly!
What if everyone laughs at you?"

His face felt hot and
his tummy twisted.

Billy pulled off his costume.

He'd just have to think
of another character
to dress up as.

But who?

*Nature Girl* was his
ABSOLUTE favourite!

All of a sudden, his book began to glow.
Then . . .

*Whoosh!*

Leaves, wind and the sound of wildlife
rushed out from the book . . .

**and Nature Girl appeared!**

"Hey, Billy!" she said. "What's up?"

"I *really* wanted to dress up as YOU today," said Billy. "But what if it makes me stand out?

What if people make fun of me?"

He looked down at the ground.
"I wish I could be brave like you,
but I'm not. I'm scared."

"Sometimes," said Nature Girl, "being BRAVE means carrying on, even when you ARE scared."

Billy nodded.
He could *try* to be brave . . .

Nature Girl smiled and helped him put his costume back on.

She *even* gave him her
very own cape!

Then in a FLASH,
she was GONE.

Later that morning, Billy stood
outside school, his heart pounding,
his hands sweaty.

What would everyone think?
Then he remembered what Nature Girl had said . . .

He would *try* to
be **BRAVE**.

Slowly, Billy pushed
open the door . . .

...and saw all his friends smiling and cheering!
Everyone LOVED his Nature Girl costume.

Billy grinned. This was going to be
the best day EVER!

# BIG BRIGHT FEELINGS

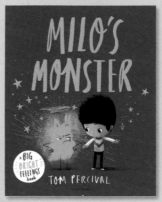

COMING SOON!

Discover the WHOLE series!